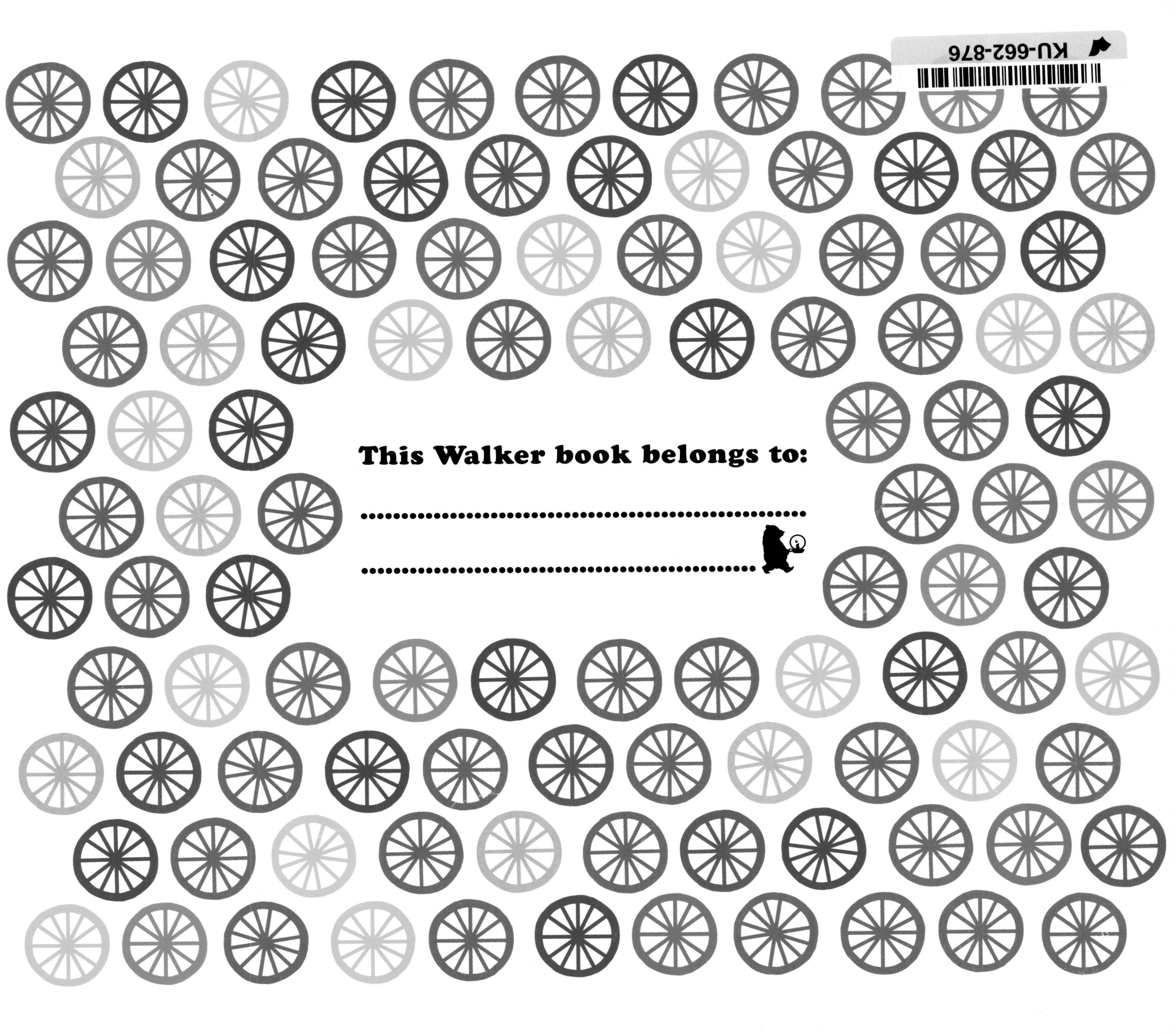

KU-662-876

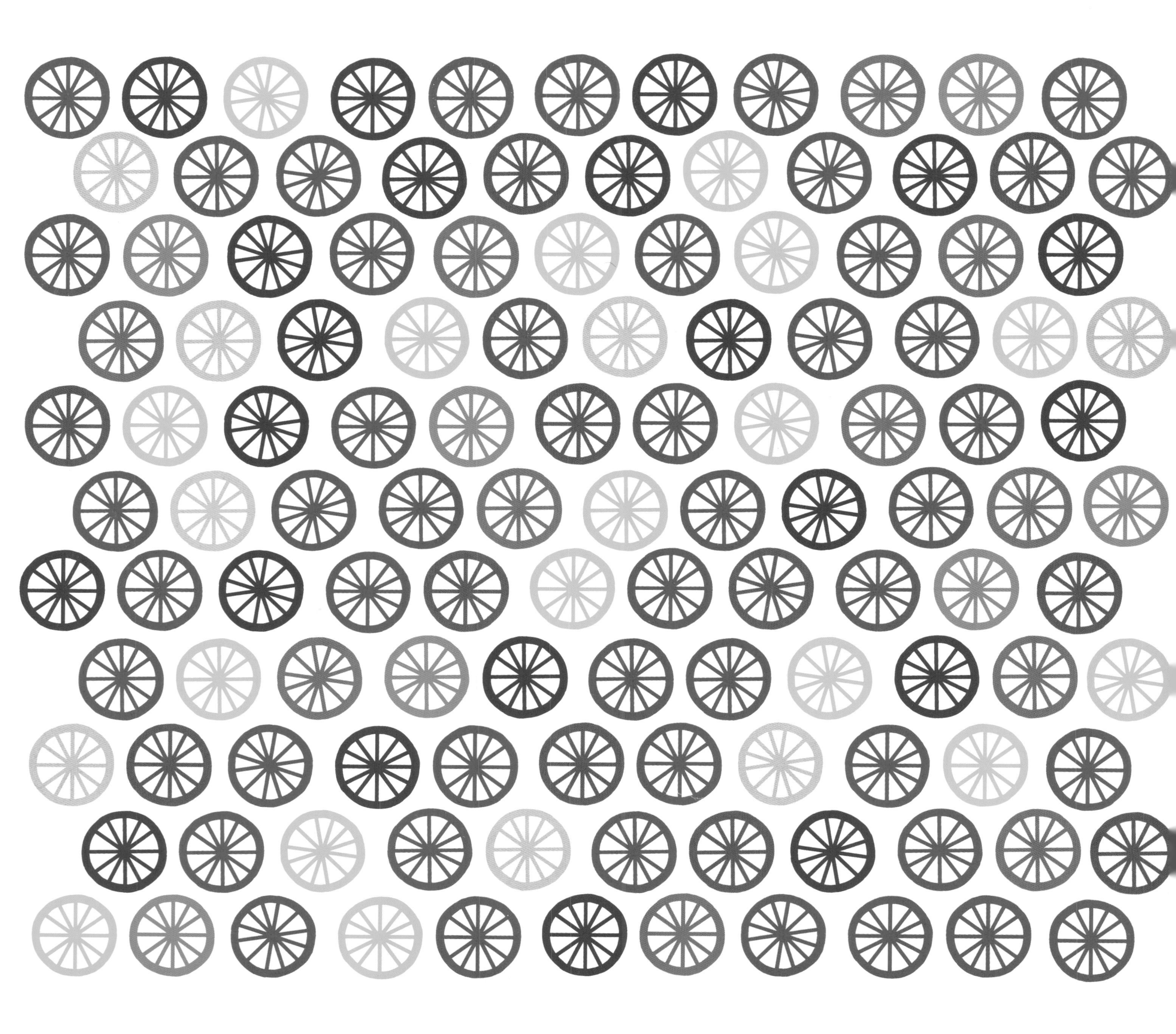

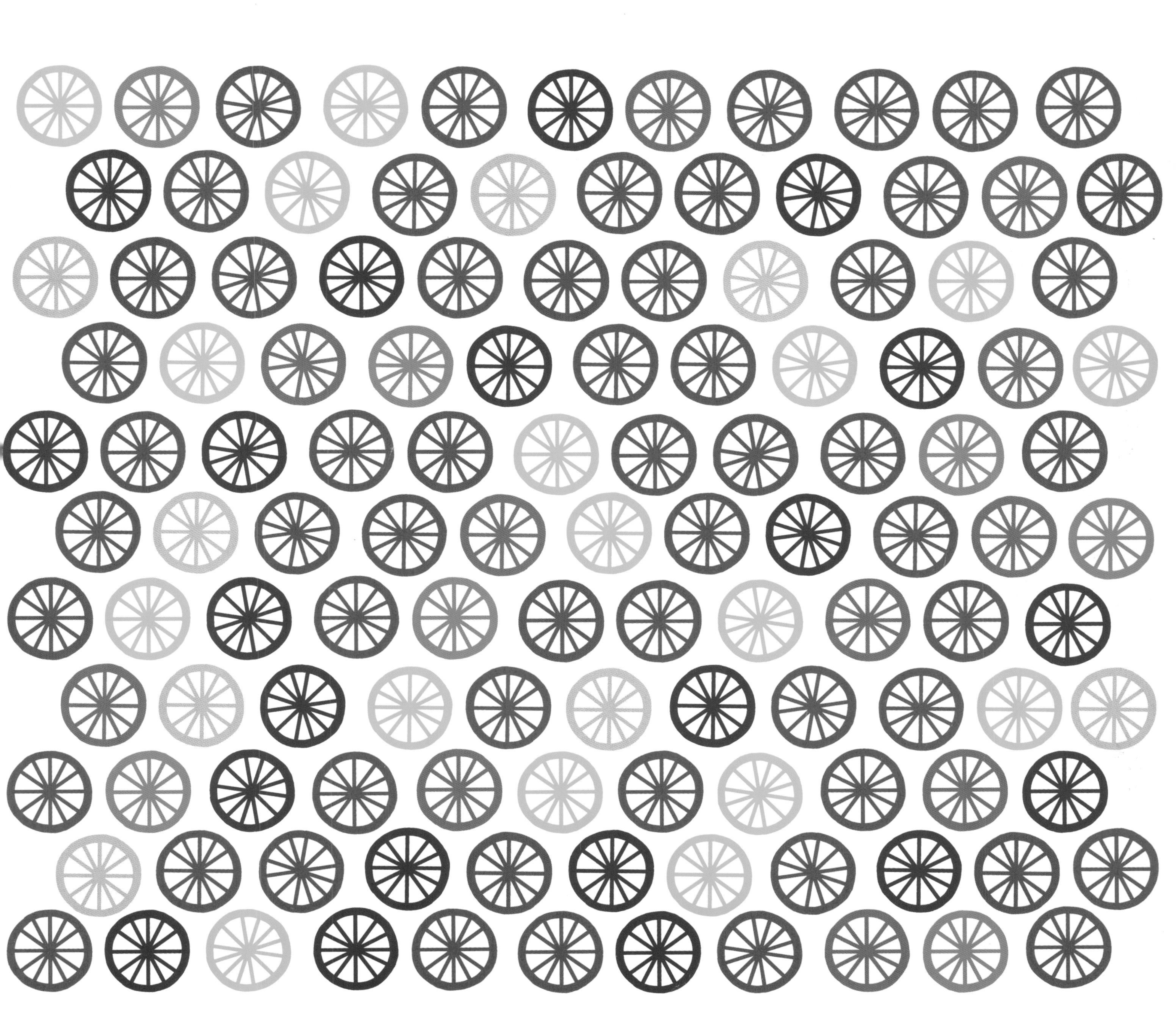

With thanks to my two guinea pigs ...
Aidan and **Beau**

First published 2007 by Walker Books Ltd
87 Vauxhall Walk, London SE11 5HJ

This edition published 2008

10 9 8 7 6 5 4

Text and illustrations © 2007 William Bee

www.williambee.com

The right of William Bee to be identified as author/illustrator of this work
has been asserted by him in accordance with the Copyright, Designs and Patents Act 1988

This book has been typeset in Frutiger

Printed in China

All rights reserved. No part of this book may be reproduced, transmitted or stored in an
information retrieval system in any form or by any means, graphic, electronic or mechanical,
including photocopying, taping and recording, without prior written permission from the publisher.

British Library Cataloguing in Publication Data:
a catalogue record for this book is available from the British Library

ISBN 978-1-4063-1247-8

www.walkerbooks.co.uk

and the train goes...

william bee

WALKER BOOKS
AND SUBSIDIARIES
LONDON • BOSTON • SYDNEY • AUCKLAND

Here is the station all noisy and full …
and the station clock goes …
"Tick tock, tickerty tock…"

and the man in the station office says …

"Hurry up! Hurry up! Any more tickets…?"

Here is the train all ready to go …
and the station master calls out …
"All aboard who are coming aboard…"

DIBNAH

DIBNAH

Here is the train leaving the station …
and its whistle blows …
“Woo woo, woo woo…”

Here is the fireman shovelling coal …
and he mutters …
"Shovel shovel, shovel shovel…"

and the train goes …

"Chuff chuff, chufferty chuff…"

Here are the ladies off to the races …

and they nitter and natter …

"Lovely cake, Doris, lovely tea, Mabel…"

and the train goes …

"Puff puff, pufferty puff…"

Here are the soldiers off on manoeuvres …
and their sergeant major bellows …
"Left, right, left, right … at ease…"

and the train goes …

"Clickerty click, clickerty clack…"

"Clickerty click, clickerty clack…"

Here is the school party off on a trip …

and the children yell …

"Please, sir, please, miss … are we there yet?"

and the train goes …

"Clickerty click, clickerty clack…"

Here are the businessmen off to the city …

and they shout …

"Faster, faster, time is money, time is money…"

and the train goes …

“Clickerty click, clickerty clack…”

“Clickerty click, clickerty clack…”

Here are the chickens off to the market …
and they go …
"Cluck cluck, cluckerty cluck…"

and the train goes …

"Clickerty click, clickerty clack…"

"Clickerty click, clickerty clack…"

Here is the guard … asleep on the job …
and he goes …
"Snore, snore, snore, snore, snore…"

and the train goes …

"Clickerty click, clickerty clack, woo wooooo…"

And here is the station all quiet and empty …
and the station clock goes …
"Tick tock, tickerty tock…"

and here is the station parrot …

and he goes …

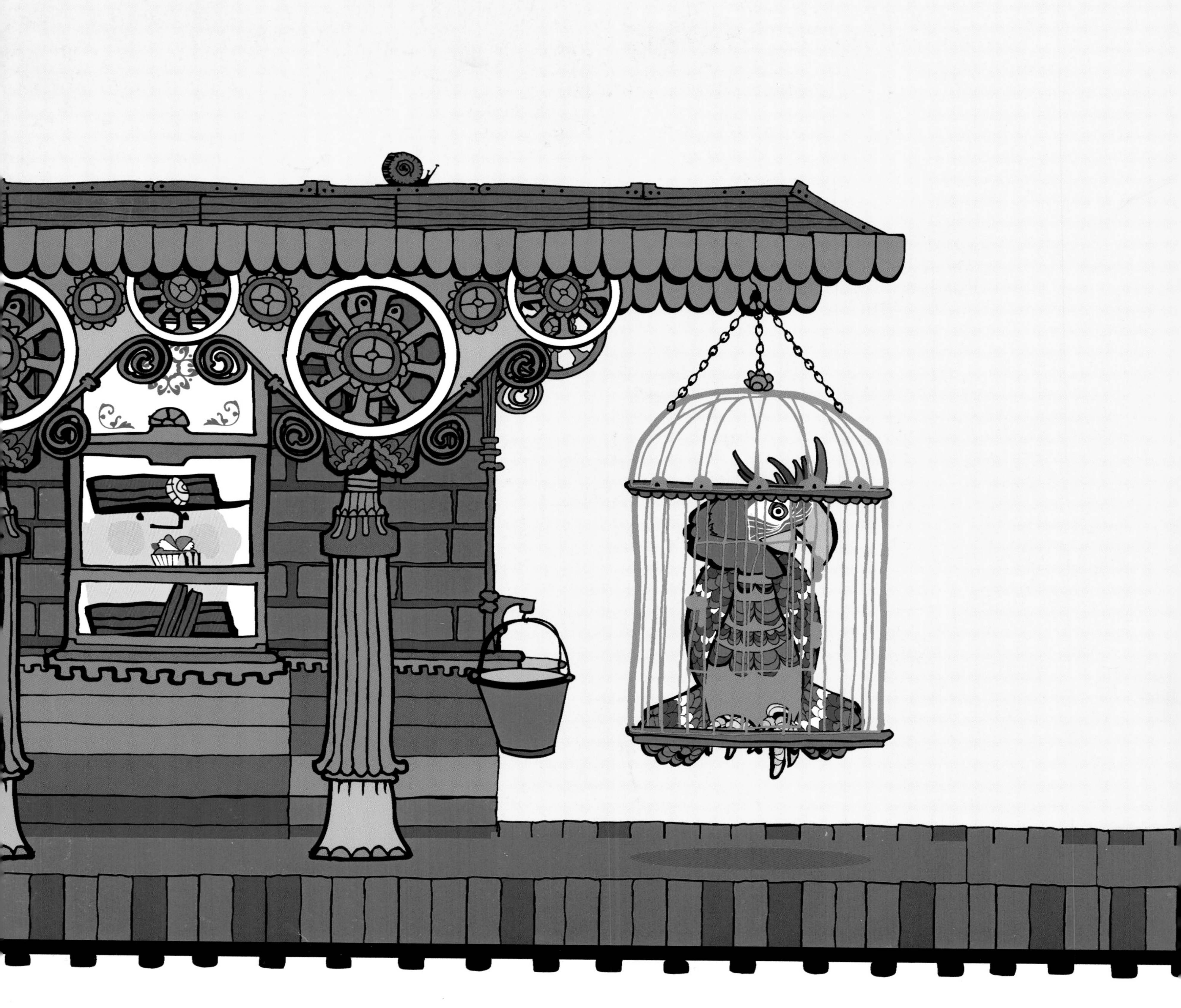

"Hurry up! Hurry up!
All aboard, all aboard,
shovel shovel, shovel shovel,
chuff chuff, chufferty chuff,
lovely cake, lovely cake,
left, right, left, right,
at ease...
Please, sir, please, miss,
time is money, time is money,
cluck cluck, cluckerty cluck,
clickerty click, clickerty clack,
squawk squawk, squawkerty squawk,
woo wooooooooooooooooooooooo....."

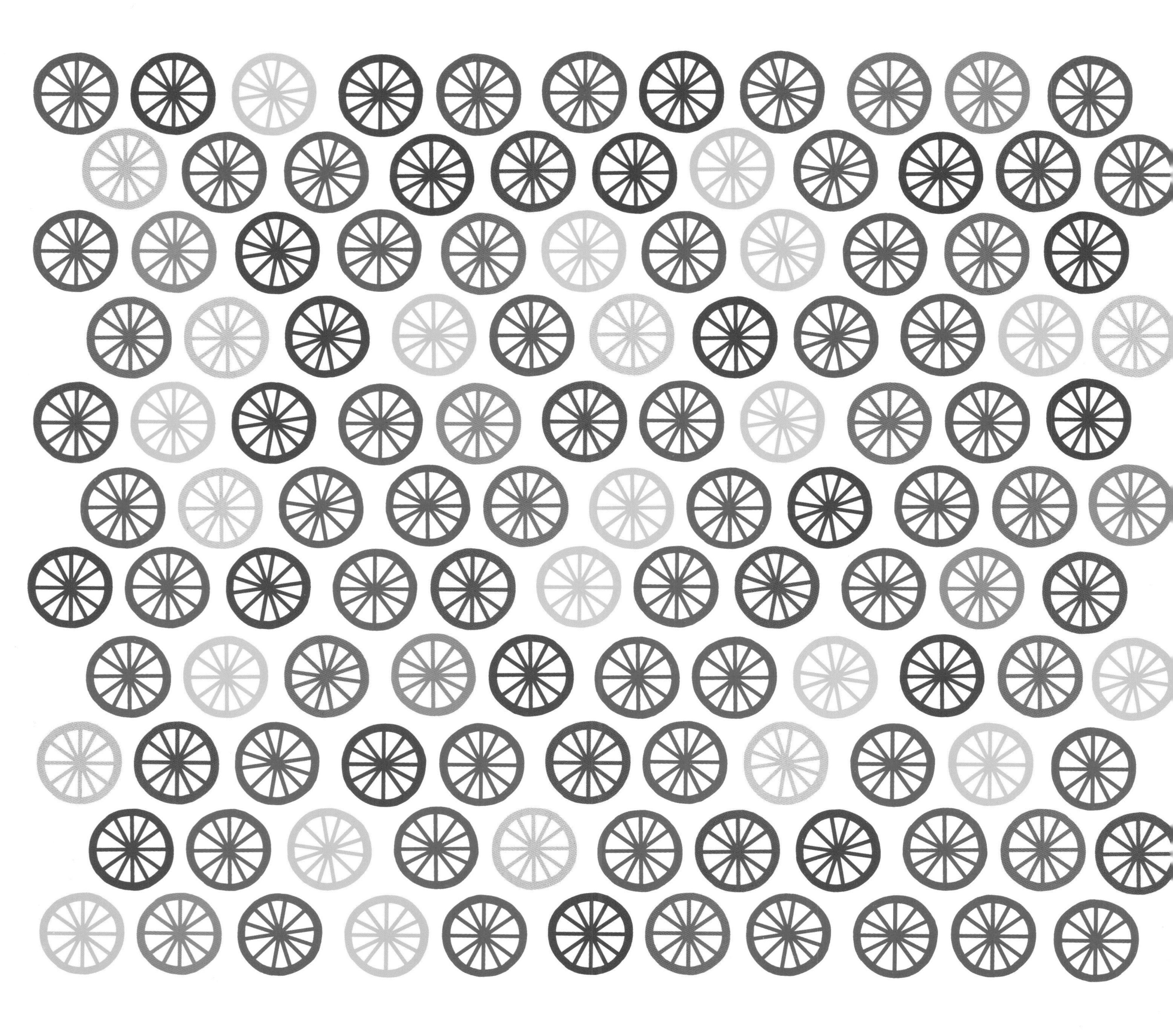

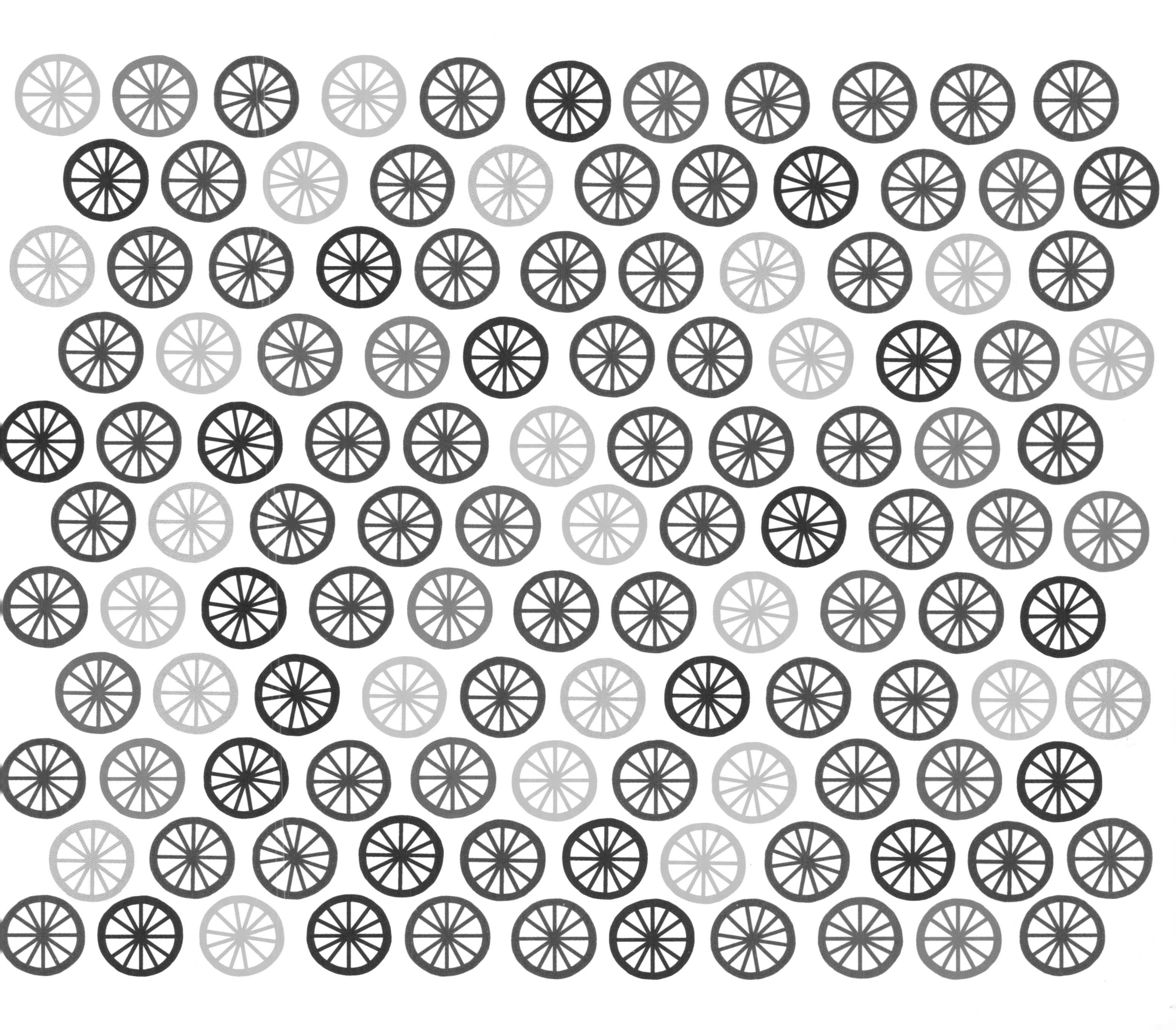

And the train goes...

Chuff chuff, chufferty chuff...
Puff, puff, pufferty puff...
Woo Wooooo!

"Cheerful and spirited ... turns the bedtime story into live entertainment." *The Independent*

"A great read-aloud book." *Junior*

ISBN 978-1-4063-1247-8

Whatever

Billy can be very difficult to please...
Whatever.

"A delightful cautionary tale." *The Sunday Telegraph*

ISBN 978-1-4063-0133-5

And the latest title from William Bee!

Beware of the Frog

Mrs Collywobbles lives on the edge of a big, dark, scary wood. The only thing protecting her from all the horrible creatures that live in it is ... her little pet frog.

ISBN 978-1-4063-0981-2